Marty™ the Millionaire

written by
Debbie Dadey

illustrated by
Meredith Johnson

To all the kids I've had the pleasure of teaching—Thanks for the millions of memories.—D.D.

For my new friend Marika, who likes to draw.—M.J.

First printing by Willowisp Press 1997.

Published by PAGES Publishing Group
801 94th Avenue North, St. Petersburg, Florida 33702

Printed in the United States of America

Willowisp Press®

2 4 6 8 10 9 7 5 3 1

ISBN 0-87406-865-7

1
Rich!

You have already won a million dollars!

Marty rubbed her eyes and read the envelope again. *You have already won a million dollars!* That's what it said all right, and the envelope had her name on it.

"I'm rich!" Marty screamed to the empty mailbox. "Just wait until Ann and Peter hear about this. Just wait until the whole city hears about it."

Marty rushed down the sidewalk to her friend Ann's house. "Ann," Marty yelled as she ran up the driveway. "Look at this!"

Ann looked up from the flower she was watering. "What's wrong with you?" she asked. "Did your brother knot your ponytail again?"

Marty shook her head and tried to catch her breath. Marty's older brother Frank liked to tease Marty. Knotting her ponytail was just one of the things he did to annoy her. The thing she hated the worst was when he called her by her real name: Martha Washington. Marty liked her nickname much better.

"No," Marty told Ann. "This is something wonderful. It has nothing to do with Frank."

Ann put down her watering can to think. "I bet your mom finally said you could get a puppy."

Marty smiled. "That'd be great, but that's not it either."

"I give up," Ann said. "What's your great news?"

"Let's go find Peter so we can tell him, too," Marty suggested.

They found Peter playing basketball in his driveway.

"I have great news," Marty told him.

Peter looked at Ann and Marty. "What?" he asked.

Marty puffed up her chest and held up the envelope. Ann's eyes got big when she read the writing.

“Oh, my gosh,” Ann said. “Can it be true?”

Marty nodded. “Your best friend is a millionaire.”

2 Shopping

"Marty," her mom yelled down the hall. "Have you finished your homework yet?"

Marty looked up from the big catalogs spread all over her bedroom floor. "Not yet," Marty called.

"You aren't goofing off, are you?" her mom asked.

"No," Marty said. "I'm doing something important."

Marty wrote two more words on her paper. She wrote *BIG TV* underneath *NEW BIKE*. Marty was making a list of everything she would buy with her million dollars. So far the list was ten pages long.

Her mom yelled down the hall again. "As soon as you finish your homework, you need to do your chores."

"Okay," Marty called back, only half-paying attention. Marty was writing a long word on her list: *LIMOUSINE*. She had found it in the yellow pages of the phone book. Marty had never actually ridden in one of the long, black cars. Marty figured limos were just for movie stars and really rich people.

Marty smiled. "Now that I'm rich, I can ride to school in style. No more walking for me. I'll even let Peter and Ann ride with me." Maybe she'd even let her brother Frank ride, too. But only if her never teased her again.

Marty shoved her math book out her way. "I'll do my homework later," she said to herself. She stretched out on the floor and added many more things to her list. She was writing *BIG BOAT* when her mom tapped on her door.

"Marty," her mom said, opening Marty's door. "Dinner is ready."

Marty looked up from the pile of catalogs and smiled. Marty started to tell her mom about the millionaire letter. She couldn't wait to see how excited her mom would be. But Marty didn't get the chance.

"Is that your homework?" Marty's mom asked.

"No," Marty told her. "I'll do that later after my chores."

"You mean you haven't done your homework *or* your chores yet?"

Marty shook her head. "I've been busy with this." Marty waved her hand over the huge piles of catalogs spread all over the floor of her room. There were even catalogs she had borrowed from Ann scattered on her bed.

Her mom frowned and folded her arms in front of her chest. "This room is a wreck. You're in big trouble for not doing your homework or your chores. You know those come first."

Marty knew when her mom folded her arms like that she meant business. "I'm sorry," Marty said. "I'll clean up this mess right away."

"Come to dinner, then you can straighten up and do your homework and chores." Marty's mom left the room shaking her head.

Marty sighed and looked at her list. Her mom wouldn't be angry anymore when she found out her daughter was rich. Marty giggled and added two more words to her list: *DIAMOND RING*. Her mom wouldn't be mad at her ever again after Marty bought her the biggest ring in all the world. "She'll be sorry she fussed at me," Marty said to herself.

"Marty!" her mom yelled.

"I'm coming," Marty called, scrambling down the hall. Marty hoped she'd get her money soon, before she got into more trouble.

3 More Trouble

"Where's your homework?" Mrs. Jones asked Marty.

Marty looked up at her third-grade teacher and gulped. Marty had meant to do her homework. She really had, but after dinner she hadn't been able to resist adding a few more pages to her list of things to buy. The next thing she knew it was morning. She'd fallen asleep in the middle of a pile of catalogs. The last thing on her list was *WATERBED.*

“I’m sorry,” Marty explained, “but I forgot my homework.”

Mrs. Jones frowned. “You will need to stay after school and do it. Don’t let this happen again, Marty.”

Marty shook her head. “No, ma’am.”

Mrs. Jones moved on to the next aisle. Marty felt a hand on her shoulder. "You're in trouble," a voice whispered behind her. It was Bobby, the class pest.

Marty tried to ignore him, but he didn't stop. "You're going to get it," Bobby said. "Mrs. Jones is going to send you to Mrs. Claret's office and then you'll be deader than an ant under a cowboy boot."

Marty shuddered. Kids said that if you went into the principal's office, you didn't come out alive. Marty turned around to give Bobby a mean look.

Bobby put his hands around his throat and pretended to choke himself. Marty felt like helping him. Instead, she stuck out her tongue.

"Marty!" Mrs. Jones snapped. "Aren't you in enough trouble for not getting your homework done?"

Marty jerked her tongue back in her mouth. "Yes, ma'am," she said.

"Then leave Bobby alone," Mrs. Jones ordered.

Marty turned around and took out her pencil. Behind her she could still hear Bobby whispering. "You're in trouble."

Marty started writing, *I don't have to worry about homework.* Then in great big letters, she wrote, *I AM A MILLIONAIRE!*

She passed the note back to Bobby and waited. Bobby studied the note. She heard him sounding out the big word. "Mill-yon-air," he muttered to himself.

"You're a liar," Bobby whispered.

"I am not," Marty whispered back angrily. When Bobby saw all the neat things she was going to buy, he'd see she really *was* a millionaire. Then he'd be sorry.

4 Stinky Rotten Tennis Shoes

"You're lying," Bobby said when they got to the playground.

"I am not," Marty told him. It was recess and lots of kids were gathered around. Ann and Peter stood right beside Marty.

“If you’re a millionaire, then why are you wearing stinky, rotten tennis shoes?” Bobby asked.

Marty looked down at her tennis shoes. They were pretty old and scuffed. One even had a rip on the side. She’d have to put new tennis shoes on her list. Marty pulled a pencil stub and a big tube of rolled-up papers from her back pocket. Quickly she wrote *SHOES* on the list.

She held the fat list up to Bobby's nose. "Would I make a list like this if I wasn't a millionaire?" she asked.

"I made a list like that once," said Allison, the prissiest girl at Tates Creek Elementary School. "It doesn't mean you're rich. It just means you'd like to be."

Lots of kids in the crowd nodded their heads. Bobby batted Marty's list away from his face. He stepped close to Marty and poked her in the stomach. "You're nothing but a big fat cat liar."

Peter pushed his glasses further up on his nose. "Don't call my friend a liar," he said.

Bobby put his face right up to Marty's. "Liar, liar, pants on fire," Bobby sang.

Ann stepped between Marty and Bobby. "She isn't lying," Ann explained. Everyone looked at Ann. They knew Marty might tell a fib or two, but Ann would never lie. She was just too nice.

"It's true," Ann explained. "I saw the letter myself. It said that Marty is a millionaire."

"Wow!" several kids gasped. They looked at Marty like she was wearing gold underwear.

One little first grader reached out and touched Marty's arm. "I touched a millionaire!" he shouted. "I touched a millionaire!" Then he danced all around the playground singing, "I touched a millionaire." In two seconds there was a long line of first graders waiting to touch Marty's arm.

"I could be a millionaire, too," Ann said with a giggle. "All I need to do is charge kids to touch your arm."

"I still don't believe you," Bobby said. Some other kids stood behind Bobby and nodded their heads. The little first graders, Peter, and Ann were the only ones who believed Marty.

Marty shrugged. "I don't care. But you're not my friend if you don't believe me. And after all, I only want to buy presents for my friends."

One short, brown-haired first-grade girl looked up at Marty with big, round eyes. "I like you, Marty. Will you buy me a new bicycle?"

Marty stuck out her tongue at Bobby. Then Marty smiled and patted the little girl on her shoulder. "Sure, I'll buy you a bicycle," Marty told her. "My friends are going to get everything they ever wanted. Just you wait and see."

5 Making a List

“I want a new skateboard,” a girl named Nancy told Marty.

Another kid grabbed Marty’s sleeve. “I’ll be your friend forever if you buy me some new skates.”

It was still recess and twenty kids squeezed close to Marty asking for presents. They each had at least three things they wanted Marty to buy them.

"Don't push," Marty told them.

Ann did her best to keep the kids from squishing Marty. "Be careful," Ann warned, "or someone could get hurt."

Peter tapped Marty on the shoulder. "You'd better do something quick before these kids go crazy."

"Ouch!" cried one little first grader. "Somebody stepped on my toe."

Marty tried to get away from the kids, but they completely surrounded her. "Listen!" Marty yelled. "If you each make out a list, I'll think about buying you some presents."

"Yip-ee!" the kids screamed and patted Marty. But to Marty, it felt more like she was being punched than patted.

"You kids had better leave Marty alone," Ann warned. "She won't get you anything if you break her arm."

"I know another reason you'd better leave Marty alone," said Peter. "Because here comes Mrs. Claret." He pointed toward a tall woman.

Immediately, all of the kids got quiet. They watched Mrs. Claret walk across the playground toward them.

Then they looked at Marty. Every kid but Marty, Peter, and Ann took off running.

"Maybe we should run, too," Ann suggested. Mrs. Claret was their school principal, and just the mention of her name was enough to make most kids faint. It was rumored that she ate troublemakers for breakfast.

Marty shook her head. "We didn't do anything wrong," she said.

Peter gulped. "I hope Mrs. Claret knows that."

"Kids," Mrs. Claret said as she came up to them, "is everything all right?"

Marty nodded. "Everything is fantastic."

Mrs. Claret folded her hands in front of her stomach and looked at Marty. It was as though she was deciding if she needed to eat her for an afternoon snack. Maybe she wasn't hungry, because she smiled and walked away.

"Whew!" Marty said as the bell rang. "It's not easy being a millionaire."

Ann giggled. "It's not easy being the friend of a millionaire, either."

All day long people kept giving Marty lists. Some lists were long and some were short, but by the end of the school day Marty's red backpack was filled with lists. Marty found Peter and Ann waiting for her outside the school.

"Thanks for waiting," Marty said. "Mrs. Jones made me finish all of my homework from yesterday. I thought I'd never get done."

Ann looked at Marty's bulging backpack as they walked home. "You look like Santa's little sister," Ann said, "but I don't think even Santa has enough money to buy everything those kids want."

Peter nodded. "You must have a list from every kid in the school. I don't know if you'll have that much money."

"Of course, I'll have enough money," Marty told them. "You can buy a lot of things with a million dollars."

"Can you buy an island of your own?" Ann asked.

"Sure," Marty said, "is that what you want?"

"No," Ann said, pointing to Marty's house, "but you might need one."

"Either that or a really fast car," Peter agreed, "to get away from all those kids."

Standing in front of Marty's house was a huge group of first and second graders. Each one of them waved a list in the air and every kid was chanting, "I want a new bike. I want a new bike."

"Oh, no," Ann said. "Now what are you going to do?"

Peter adjusted his backpack and looked at Marty. "You may have to change your name."

Marty wanted to run, but she gulped instead. It wasn't all the kids in her yard that worried her. It was her mother standing on the porch. Her mother's arms were folded in front of her and she was yelling, "Martha Washington!"

6
Grounded

"Grounded," Marty muttered as she fell onto her bed. "How can I shop for presents if I'm grounded?"

Marty's mom yelled down the hall, "You'd better get your homework done right away, young lady! I still can't believe you told those kids you'd buy them bikes. What in the world were you thinking? Do you think money grows on trees?"

Marty knew better than to argue with her mom. She unzipped her backpack and dug through all the lists. Her math book was at the bottom. With a sigh, Marty pulled it out and started working on page thirty-six.

She was half-finished when the phone rang. "Marty," her mom called. "Peter is on the phone."

Marty ran into the kitchen and grabbed the portable phone. Her mom held up two fingers. "You can talk for two minutes and that's all," her mom said. "You're still in big trouble."

"Yes, ma'am," Marty said with a nod. She carried the phone into her room before talking to Peter.

"Hi, Peter," Marty said.

Peter's voice was soft over the phone. "Did you get in big trouble?" he asked.

"My mom grounded me for the rest of my life," Marty said.

"She did that when you put syrup in your brother's ballcap and she forgot about it after a few days," Peter told her. "I'm sure she'll forget about this, too."

Marty frowned. She had done that when she was only four, and she'd grown up a lot since then. "She was really mad," she told Peter. "I think she meant it this time."

"I've been thinking about that letter you got," Peter said.

"You mean my millionaire letter?" Marty asked.

"Did you get any *other* letters?" Peter asked.

"Well, no," Marty admitted.

"I want to see that letter," Peter told her.

"But I'm grounded," Marty reminded him.

"That's okay," Peter said. "I'll come up to your window and you can show it to me there. I may have some more bad news for you."

"All right. Come on over. But be quiet. I'm in enough trouble already."

She turned off the phone and looked for the letter. Why did Peter want to see it anyway? What bad news could be worse than being grounded?

7
The Letter

"Pssst! Psssst!"

The rest of her homework forgotten, Marty was busy looking at all the lists kids had given her. She heard a noise.

"Pssst! Psssst!"

"These kids are greedy," Marty said to herself, ignoring the sound. "They want stuff they don't even need."

YOU HAVE ALREADY WON
A MILLION DOLLARS

"Pssst! Pssst!"

Marty heard the noise again. This time she remembered it must be Peter outside her window. Marty ran over to the window and opened it.

"Hi," Marty said to Peter. "Thanks for coming. But we have to be quiet or my mom will kill me. I can't have friends over when I'm grounded."

Peter was all business. He pushed his glasses further up on his nose, then reached out a hand. "Where's the millionaire letter?"

"Isn't it exciting?" Marty asked him as she handed it over. "I can buy whatever I want."

Peter didn't say anything. He just took the envelope and studied it.

"I'm going to buy presents for everybody," Marty told him. "You'll have to tell me what you'd like and I'll write it down. I'm still looking at all the lists the kids at school gave me." Marty pointed to the huge pile of papers on her bed.

Peter looked at the lists. Then he looked at Marty. Without a word he looked at the envelope again. Next, he opened the envelope and took out some brightly colored papers.

"Haven't you read the letter yet?" Peter asked.

Marty's face got a little red. "Well, I've been busy deciding how to spend my money. Is the letter important?"

Peter coughed and held up the letter. "See this little tiny print?"

Marty leaned out the window and squinted to read the little print. "It's just about too little to read," she complained.

Peter nodded. "It's little, but important. I'm afraid I have some bad news for you."

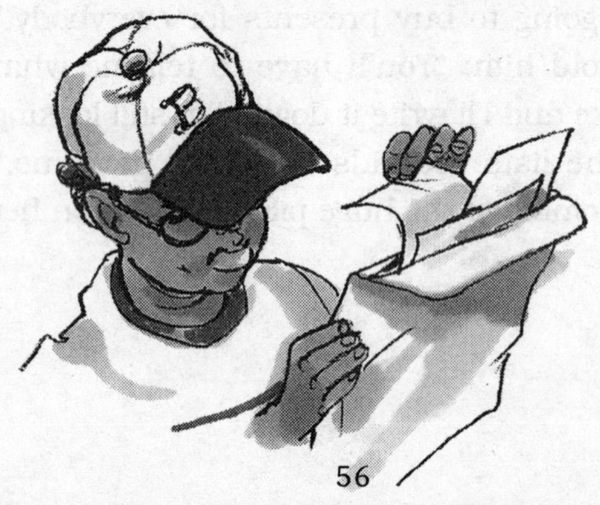

Marty and Peter heard a noise and they jumped. Marty turned around to see her mother standing in the doorway.

"I have some bad news, too," Marty's mom told her. "You're in BIG trouble!"

8
Poor Little Rich Girl

"It's not fair," Marty complained as she and Ann walked to school the next morning. "My mother won't even listen to a word I say."

Ann shrugged her shoulders. "She's just mad because you didn't do your chores or your homework. And it didn't help that you promised half the kids at school a new bike."

"I couldn't help all those things," Marty explained. "I've been really busy. Looking at everybody's list took me all night long. Being a millionaire is definitely not as easy as it looks."

Ann patted Marty on the shoulder. "It's hard to feel sorry for someone who can buy anything she wants."

Marty looked up the sidewalk. A whole group of first graders were rushing toward her. "Marty!" they yelled. "Will you buy us some presents?"

"Would you feel sorry for me if I'm crushed to death by a mob of greedy little first graders?" Marty asked Ann. "They're nothing but a bunch of parasites."

Ann took one look at the swarm of kids. "There's only one thing to do," she told Marty. "Run!"

Ann and Marty ran around the kids like pro football players. They didn't stop running until they were at the school door.

Marty panted. "We've got to find someplace to hide or they'll never leave us alone."

Ann nodded. "I wish Peter was here. He's good at finding hiding places."

"Why did he have to pick this morning to go to the dentist?" Marty asked. "He said he had some bad news for me. I wonder what it is?"

Ann looked around the corner. "Marty," Ann said, "I've got some bad news, too."

"What?" Marty asked.

"The greedy parasites are here and if we don't move fast, we'll be squashed flatter than a bug under a semi-truck!" Ann yelled.

9
Abdominal Snowman

"What happened to you?" Peter asked Marty after school.

Ann looked at Marty and giggled. "You look like the Abdominal Snowman." Marty was white from her head to her toes and a cloud of white dust hung in the air around her. They were outside the school near the trash cans and dumpster.

"I had to clean the chalkboard erasers for the whole third grade," Marty told them. "And besides, it's the *Abominable* Snowman." She clapped two erasers together and white specks of chalk flew everywhere.

"Why did you offer to do that?" Peter asked.

"Mrs. Claret made me," Marty said sadly, "because I didn't get my homework finished two days in a row."

Ann chewed on a fingernail before saying, "You'd better start getting your homework before Mrs. Claret has you scrubbing toilets."

"Being a millionaire is no picnic," Marty said with a sigh. "I've never been in so much trouble in my life. And I can't even walk on the playground without getting mobbed by millionaire-mad first graders."

Peter and Ann picked up some erasers and clapped them together to help Marty. "You make being a millionaire sound terrible," Ann told her. "I think it would be great."

"Is being grounded great?" Marty asked.

Ann shook her head. "No."

"Is being in trouble with the principal great?" Marty asked, as she banged two erasers together.

Ann shook her head. "No."

"Is breathing chalk dust great?" Marty asked.

Peter coughed. "No, it's horrible."

Ann put her erasers down on a trash can and tried to brush the chalk off her hands. "You make it sound like you wish you'd never won the money in the first place."

Marty looked at the thick coat of white chalk powder on her hands. "I'm sick of the whole thing."

Peter put down his erasers and touched Marty on the arm. "Do you wish you weren't a millionaire?"

Marty nodded. "It's terrible. I just want things were back the way they used to be when I was plain, ordinary Marty Washington."

Peter smiled and pushed his glasses further up his nose. A little spot of white chalk dust stuck on his glasses right between his eyes. "I have some good news for you then," he said.

"I thought you had bad news for me," Marty told him as she gathered up all the erasers.

"It was bad news, but now it's good news," Peter said.

Ann chewed on her fingernail and Marty held the erasers close to her. "Well," Marty said, "what's the news?"

"You're not a millionaire," Peter said.

10 The Contest

Marty dropped the erasers and glared at Peter. "You take that back!" she yelled.

"I thought you didn't want to be a millionaire," Peter told her.

"I was upset," Marty said.

Ann patted Marty's shoulder. "You're a little upset right now."

"You'd be upset too if someone just took a million dollars away from you," Marty said.

"You never had a million dollars," Peter explained. "Let me see your letter again and I'll show you."

Marty pulled the letter out of her backpack. Peter pointed to the small print and read it out loud. "'You could win a million dollars by filling out this form before May the first.'"

"You mean I have to fill out the form before I get the money?" Marty asked.

"You have to fill out the form *and* win the contest," Peter said. "Someone else could win."

"That's not fair," Marty said.

Ann wiped her chalky hands on her pants. "Maybe it's for the best," she told Marty. "After all, you said you didn't like being a millionaire."

"But that was before," Marty said. "I wasn't a real millionaire. I'm going to fill out that form and win. This time I'll be a REAL millionaire. It'll be much better."

Peter and Ann shook their heads and smiled. Marty sat down on the sidewalk with chalkboard erasers all around her. She took out a pencil and started filling out the form.

Marty looked up at her friends and smiled. "When I win, we can go shopping, and I'll buy you whatever you want."

"Oh, no," Ann groaned. "Here we go again!"

Peter pointed to a group of first graders heading toward them. "You're right. They're ready to mob us again."

Marty looked at the millionaire letter and then at the kids rushing toward her with their lists in hand. She smiled at Peter and Ann. "You guys were right. Being a millionaire is a little too exciting for me. I think it's time to be the regular Marty Washington again." Marty held up the letter and ripped it down the middle.

"Good-bye, Marty the Millionaire!" Peter said.

"Thank goodness," Ann said. "I like the normal Marty best of all."

"Me, too," Marty said. Then she giggled and tossed the letter into a nearby trash can. "Me, too."

About the author

Debbie Dadey is a former teacher and librarian. She loves being a full-time writer and visiting schools.

She lives in Aurora, Illinois, with her husband Eric. They have two children, Nathan and Rebekah. The family also has a puppy named Bailey.

Marty the Millionaire is Debbie Dadey's forty-seventh book for young readers.

About the illustrator

Meredith Johnson works as an art director creating lots and lots of TV commercials for Barbie® and Ken®. But she really likes to draw pictures for kids' books best.

Meredith and her husband Larre live in Flintridge, California. Their son Matt wants to be a millionaire when he grows up. Casey, their daughter, says she might marry one!